CH00841785

THE RAINBOW SCHOOL

BILLY AND THE SPARKLING SOCKS

(Second Edition)

By Julie Day

Published by Julie Day at Amazon

Copyright 2016 Julie Day

Cover and illustrations by Rachel

Lawston of Lawston Designs

This book is licensed for your personal enjoyment only. This book may not be resold or given away to other people. If you would like to share this book with another person, please purchase an additional copy for each recipient. If you're reading this book and did not purchase it, or it was not purchased for your use only, then please return to where you purchased it and buy your own copy. Thank you for respecting the hard work of this author.

This book is dedicated to my mum, Jean Day. My mum has been through all the ups and downs with me that having Asperger's Syndrome brings, and was with me when I was diagnosed with Asperger's Syndrome in 2011. Thank you, Mum, for being there for me.

Chapter One

"School again tomorrow. Can't wait,"
Casper Bottomsby said to his ten-year-old
brother, Billy. "Oh yes, how could I
forget? I got a gold star in geography on
Friday." He beamed.

Billy gave a smile, and bowed his head.
Only then, when no one could see, did a
scowl appear on his face.

"What's up, Billy? Jealous of my good
mark?" Casper said, grinning.

Billy tried to stay silent by clamping his mouth shut, but he failed as his face heated up and his cheeks start bulging out. He raised his head and faced his brother with a glare. "Stop bragging," he said. "It's boring. You're boring!"

"You're jealous," Casper said. "Jealous cos you don't talk to your classmates. Never mind, eh."

"I am good at something!" Billy shouted. He stood up, scraping his chair back.

"What?" Casper challenged him.

"Don't know. I will find out."

"Boys, please stop it. Billy, sit down and finish your dinner."

His mum touched his arm. He wiggled his shoulder, so she dropped her hand away. He hated being touched.

"Sorry," she said. She gave him a thumbs-up sign instead.

He looked up at her. He put up a hand to show 'What do you mean by saying it's OK?'

"OK. Let's try what I know you like and understand. More words." She went to the cupboard. She put a piece of paper and a pen on the table, then drew a smile on the paper.

He understood a smiley face. He drew a smile, too.

"Only if he," Billy pointed at Casper, "shuts up about school. He thinks," and Billy prodded Casper's head, "he's the only one who is good at school. Well, Casper, I'm going to show you that I can be good, too." He pointed at himself with a finger. He drew a big smile on the paper. "Me," he said.

"You wanna bet?" Casper held out a hand.

"Yes." Billy shook Casper's hand. "I bet you that by the end of the week I'll be as good as or better than you at one lesson. And I'll have friends, like you."

"You're on."

Billy drew a straight line, an arrow, and a smile on the paper. Pointing at the straight line, he said, "You." At the smile, he said, "Me."

They both sat down and finished their dinner.

Every now and then Billy glanced up at his brother, who was smiling. With each smile, Billy became even more determined to beat his brother at school. His breathing got faster and faster at the thought. He just had to work out which lesson, though. He knew his classmates thought he was weird because he didn't speak to them or out loud in lessons, afraid that others would laugh at what he said. There had to be one lesson where he could learn how to talk to his friends properly. He'd go to each lesson, listen and learn that way. Now that was a plan.

He sat opposite his mum, and when he caught her eye, she drew a smile in the air this time. But this smile didn't look like a normal smile. It looked more like a tick than telling him to be happy, and she was waving a wand about.

At six 'o clock, Billy sat in his chair, watching the News. "That's Sophie Raworth," he said.

"You're weird, gazing at the presenters," Casper said, pulling a face.

"Leave Billy alone," their mum told him. "Let him watch TV."

When it was bedtime, he went upstairs to get changed. On the way up, he thought about the challenge. Casper had started it by bragging about his marks. He mimicked Casper: "Mum, I got a gold star. Mum, I got a gold star." All he ever did, Billy thought, was brag about what good marks he got at school. It had got annoying, which was why he'd had to say something tonight.

He tried to stop feeling sorry for himself. He couldn't help it if he didn't chat to others or choose to speak out loud in class. He had tried, but found it so hard and scary, so he always clammed up.

Looking in the bathroom mirror, Billy saw his shoulders droop. Even his clothes were boring: his pyjamas were a drab stripey grey. And his hair was boring. It was so flat, like it had been poured over his head and had stuck there. He ruffled it with his hands. But even that didn't work. His hair stood up, then went back to its usual flatness. Casper would find it funny, but he didn't. Even his eyes were average. Just the normal brown ones. They didn't sparkle or shine at all.

Billy sighed. He looked normal, but he knew he wasn't. It wasn't his fault he had autism and found it hard to make friends.

In his bedroom, Billy found a pen and some paper from his schoolbag. He wrote a list of all his lessons. One by one, he'd see what he was good at and either give it a tick or a cross.

Tucked up in bed later, Billy watched his mum get his clean clothes out for the next day.

She placed them neatly on his chair. As she did, he was sure he heard her whispering something. To his clothes? And she was drawing a smile over them, too? Why would she want his school socks to be happy?

"Mum," he called.

"Yes, Billy?" She turned round to face him.

"What were you saying then?"

"Oh that. Just wishing good night to your clothes."

Eh? His mum could be strange at times. Talking to his clothes, and drawing smiles over them. Mad.

"Goodnight, Billy," she said. "Don't worry about school. It will be okay." He was sure that she winked at him as she drew a smile in the air. She didn't say anything else, so maybe it was a trick of the light.

"Night, Mum," he said.

As his mum shut the door, he thought,

I hope it will be okay. I will be good as Casper.

I will be a success. Tomorrow, I will do my

best to be good at something. And I'll do it

despite my disability, or because of it.

Tomorrow will be the start of a new life; one

where I will be more confident and chat to my

classmates, make friends. You wait, Casper.

Chapter Two

The next morning when Billy stepped into the playground, his socks tickled his legs, like ants crawling on his skin. He recalled his mum talking to them the night before. Had she put a spell on them?

He bent down and touched his leg. No. No insects crawling on it. *Forget it. I'm at school. I am going to be good at a lesson today.*

Then things got weirder. As he thought he'd be good at a lesson, Billy saw the spot where he was standing in the playground go black, like a hole appearing, and as it got bigger and bigger, inside it turned into ... the sparkly colours of the rainbow.

Through the rainbow, Billy saw shadows. They changed into people. It looked like a children's TV programme. Full of bright colours and shapes all over the walls. And the shapes were ... rainbows.

Then he noticed the words on the wall.

They spelt, 'Story Time with ..." With

who, he wondered. Someone was in front

of the rest of the words, hiding them.

That person moved, and Billy saw his

name: Billy.

"Story Time with Billy," he read. Billy who? And then a small figure came into the picture. Billy blinked fast. No way! That looked like ... him. How could he be a presenter with autism? He had trouble talking to his brother, let alone to a group of people. A small voice told him, 'Think about Sophie Raworth.'

A bell ringing broke the scene. Billy shook his head. Gazing around him, he saw he was back at school. His teacher, Miss Murray, was beside him. She said, "Are you coming in, Billy?"

"Oh yes. Miss?" he said.

"Yes, Billy?"

"There was a hole in the ground." He shook his head.

"Was there?"

"Yes, and in it I saw myself." He glanced up at her.

"Really?"

Billy chewed his lip. Was Miss Murray teasing him or did she believe him? He couldn't tell.

"Yes, I saw myself as a storyteller on TV." He watched for a reaction, but there was no sign of surprise.

"That's good, Billy." As they reached the classroom, she said, "Remember what you saw, Billy." She winked at him.

What was that about? As he entered the classroom, a thought occurred to him. Miss Murray had smiled when she winked, like the smiles his mum drew for him.

His first lesson was numeracy. It wasn't his best subject, but he'd give it a go. As he thought this, the socks scratched him and he wiggled his foot to get rid of the feeling.

What are you telling me? he silently asked them. *That I can be good, if I give it a go?* Then he remembered what Miss Murray had said, and he thought about what he'd seen in the hole.

He picked up a pencil from the neat line of pencils along his desk. Slowly, he wrote out the sums from the board into his book. He looked at the numbers. Could he make a story out of them?

Miss Murray said, "Class, I will give you thirty minutes to work out the answers. Starting now."

Billy bent his head and put pen to paper. There was a rainbow of colours shining round the pen like he'd seen in the playground. He'd give it a go, anyway.

He used his fingers to count.

One by one he did the sums, then wrote out his answers.

When Miss Murray called, "Time's up," he put down his pencil in the space for it on his desk, happy that for once he'd done them all.

But as Miss Murray asked a boy or girl to give the answers, his smiled turned into a frown. At first he gave himself a tick, then a cross and another and another. He had only got one sum right.

He dropped his head. He heard Miss Murray say, "Put your hand up if you got half of the sums right." Billy dropped his head more when he saw that half of his class had their hands up.

He heard titters around him. There was a whisper of, "Billy is being dumb again." Billy looked to see who had started the whispers. He groaned. It was Alistair, or Anxious Alistair, as the class called him because he always seemed to be biting his fingernails after he spoke.

Billy leant forwards more over his desk. Was he seeing what he thought he saw? Yes, he was. There above Alistair's head was a ... sparkly rainbow. What did that mean? That Alistair would start seeing things one day like he did?

Alistair must've spotted him looking at him, because he shouted out, "What you staring at?" Billy saw him chew a fingernail.

Billy bent his head back over his book.

He took out his list and gave maths a cross.

"That's enough. I won't have any teasing from any of you," Miss Murray told the class.

At the end of the lesson, when the bell rang out, and it was just him and Miss Murray, he looked at her.

"I tried my best, miss," he said, bowing his head.

"I'm sure you did, Billy. You'll get better."

He hoped so.

He wasn't that good at numbers, but he still had all the other lessons to go to. Maybe he could try harder in those to find something he could talk about. He wanted to win and wipe that grin off Casper's face. He'd show Casper that he was good at something, even if he had Asperger's and couldn't communicate with others, especially groups like his class.

Chapter Three

Then came literacy.

He enjoyed this lesson as he liked writing and making up stories with words. Maybe because he liked the lesson he could do better at this.

His socks tickled him again, but this time it was more like the ants were dancing on his skin than just crawling. If his mum had made the socks magical with a spell, could they hear what he thought? Worth a try.

You think cos I like it, I can make it work for me, he thought to his socks. They tickled him even more. Yes, they'd heard him. *Okay, I'll give it a go.*

Writing on the board, Miss Murray said, "Today, we are going to write in our books ten long words. Then I want you to practise writing them so you are used to them and how they are spelled. Then I want you to write two short paragraphs. So, that is one paragraph with five words, and the other with the rest of the words. Good luck, and we'll read them out at the end of the lesson."

Billy read the words and slowly wrote out: television, neighbour, bubblegum, pavement, cushion, watching, eating, walking, driving, chewing.

He realised what Miss Murray had done. She had written five doing words to go with the other words.

He wrote them until he had a full page of them in neat lines. Then he paired the words with one another. He had an idea. He had a story.

As he looked at the words again, his exercise book shone silver. He felt his body go as light as a feather, and all around him sparkled different colours, which turned into a rainbow. Then the rainbow vanished.

Billy closed his eyes, then opened them. He gasped at what he saw. Where was he? This wasn't school. This looked like the same TV show he'd seen in that hole.

The man he'd seen before said, "Billy will be here shortly." Then, "Ah, here he is now, boys and girls." He turned to face Billy.

He had been seen. How? This world wasn't real, although he was.

The man waved him over.

Billy walked like he'd been drawn to the man, as though he was a magnet.

"It's your time, Billy," the man said. Then he walked away, leaving Billy facing the children.

Now what? But then he felt a burst of
energy beat through him, from his toes to
his head. He knew what he had to do.
Instead of feeling his usual nervous self,
he opened his mouth and called, "Hello,
children," waving at them.

As he told a story, he acted out the actions. It was like he was miming them, as though he was seeing the images around him, feeling they were real and he was there and doing the actions at the scene and not in the studio. When he had finished his story, Billy knew that was what he had to do to not be boring telling his stories.

When he thought this, Billy felt a fizzy sensation in his mouth. It was like he'd got a mouthful of Cola, and it was popping.

He felt his body go light once more, and his world go all silver and sparkly. His socks must've heard his thoughts, and were taking him back to school.

The next second he was back in the classroom. The popping had calmed down, but had left a buzzing instead, which then went to his head. Billy started to feel the popping in his mind, like lights all being turned on inside him.

He glanced around him. No one had seen him disappear. They were all still writing. That's what he should do.

As the images were there in his mind, the words popped into his head. It was like his pen had taken over his hand, and the ink inside it was flowing out like a river, but into words.

Once Billy had written his story, he read it through to himself. It *was* a good story.

His socks tickled him. *Ah. They must think so, too,* he thought. They tickled him when he had a good idea or was learning. Like when he told them he'd be good at a lesson.

"Okay, write one more word, then put your pens down," Miss Murray told them.

Billy put his pen down. And in his excitement, he put it on another pen, causing his row to roll. Oh no. They'd go out of order now, spoiling his routine of how he used them. He spent the next minute lining them all up again. He had his routine and if it got out of tune, then he'd get confused and bumble again, which would agitate him, causing a scene. He hated making scenes. They brought attention to him, meaning that others would laugh at him.

Miss Murray went from one table to another, getting them to read out their stories, until she got to his.

"Okay, who wants to read their story?" she asked, looking around the room.

Billy looked round his table at the others. No one had their hand up. He took a deep breath, then raised his hand.

"Billy?" she said, smiling at him.

"I've written one with all the words," he said.

"Gotta hear this," Alistair called. "Give us a laugh, Billy. Go on. Bet you couldn't if you tried."

Billy looked over at Alistair. Yes. The rainbow had appeared again.

Miss Murray said, "Go ahead," winking at him. That same shining and sparkly one that made her look excited. And now he thought about it, like the sparkles from the mysterious world. Was she excited at his bravery?

Billy stood up, holding his book in front of him. The book trembled in his hand. You can do it, he told himself. Think of the TV world. He took a deep breath for a few seconds, and when he felt calm, he began.

"I was watching television," he said. One boy yawned out loud and put his hand over his mouth, another put his head on his arms as though he was going to sleep, and a third called out, "Boring."

Billy stopped. Should he carry on?

Then he felt his socks ... move on him?

And he saw his pen glow silver, just like

his exercise book had when he began

writing. He knew that he had to carry on.

So he did, saying the long words louder

than the others. "I was watching

television when I saw my neighbour walk

past outside. He seemed to be chewing

bubblegum. He was so busy chewing that

he didn't see our other neighbour driving

his car out of his space as he went to cross

the pavement. But I had." As he read, he

got into his story, waving his hands about for emphasis to his words.

"I went to the front door to warn him, but I didn't see the cushion on the floor, and I tripped up …." he pretended to trip, stretching his arms out as though falling … "and the sweet I'd been eating flew out of my mouth." Billy stopped. "That's as far as I got, Miss."

There was silence. Oh no, everyone thought it was boring, or bad, or both. Then he looked at Miss Murray. She was smiling. Then the room filled with applause. Billy grinned as he saw even Alistair was clapping.

When it quietened down, Miss Murray said, "Oh, Billy. That was good. Really good. I didn't know you could write and act like that. Well done. You get a silver star for that."

Billy smiled, too. He hadn't known he had it in him, either.

At the end of the lesson, when Billy received his star, he saw Miss Murray draw a smile next to it. Eh? It so looked like the ones his mum drew for him. And when he looked at it closer outside the classroom, he saw it was exactly the same as the ones his mum did for him. Not only that, but he saw rainbows shining around it, just like the ones he'd seen in the mysterious world. What did it all mean?

He took out his list and gave literacy a tick. He now knew that he was good at that lesson, so he would work harder in it. He could communicate better with people by writing things down. Mmm ... that was something to think about.

Chapter Four

His next lesson was Design and Technology. *Could he make something good today?*

"Okay. Team up in pairs. We will be baking choc chip cookies," Miss Applebee said.

Billy watched as his class went into pairs. He was on his own again, standing alone by Miss Applebee's table like he usually was. His shoulders drooped.

"Oh, Billy," Miss Applebee said, joining him. "I'll be your team-mate today. Come on, let's bake cookies."

Billy helped his teacher put the mixture together in the bowl, then pour it into a tray.

Miss Applebee put the tray into the oven. "They should be ready in thirty minutes," she said, putting her oven gloves on the side.

After thirty minutes, everyone took out their cookies.

A few minutes later, they all tried them, and the room became full of "umms" and "aahs."

But Billy took one bite of his – and chewed and chewed and chewed. His jaw ached with all the chewing, so he gulped down the last bit of the cookie. Miss Applebeee had a bite, too, and he could see that she was having trouble eating it; her mouth was going round and round.

"If you don't like it, don't eat it," he told Miss Applebee.

Miss Applebee chewed one more time, then said, "That was ... okay. It tastes ... okay."

That word again. Okay. Not bad, not great or yummy, but okay.

He dropped his head and he felt his face heat up with the shame.

So he wasn't good at baking. *Was it because he hadn't told himself he'd be good at it? And his socks hadn't tickled him. Or was it because it just wasn't his thing?*

Alistair guffawing brought him out of his thoughts.

He glared at Alistair.

Alistair said, "So, you're not good at this, Billy. Gives some hope to us."

Billy saw that the rainbow had lost some of its sparkle. Did it mean that it didn't like Alistair teasing him? He thought, You'll eat your words, Alistair. I'll bet you I'll make you laugh this week.

When no one was looking, Billy got out his list. He gave Design and Technology a cross. He couldn't bake, but he could write a story. Food for thought, that was.

Chapter Five

Next was geography.

He was interested in different places, so he might be good at this.

His socks heard his thoughts. He felt them tickle him, like those ants were jumping up and down ... in excitement?

Miss Murray said, "As it's the last lesson of the term, it will be quiz time today. I have put pictures of different animals with different countries on your table. I want you to match the animal to its country. You have thirty minutes to do this, then we will find the answers. Good luck. You can start now." She pressed a watch in her hand.

Billy looked at the animal pictures. There was a camel, a panda, a koala, an antelope and a lion. The countries were: China, Australia and South and East Africa and Egypt.

He gazed at the animals, then the map and had an idea.

As soon as his pen touched paper, it shone silver. Then the book begun to sparkle with the rainbow colours. Would he disappear again?

He felt his body go light. So yes, he guessed he was about to visit that mysterious world. It felt like he was twirling around and around through a tunnel of rainbow sparkles until ... he blinked.

His blinking must have stopped the flight he was in, as he found he was now facing a cameraman.

Standing up, Billy felt the fizzing again. This time it was like he had a mouthful of fizzy drinks and they were tingling, from his tongue to the roof of his mouth.

Behind him appeared a huge screen, and a picture of a lion came into focus. The lion roared, and when he heard the noise, Billy, too, roared, making the children in front of him laugh. The next animal was a panda. This was what he had to write about at school. Someone must've read his thoughts, for as soon as he thought about school, the scene began to change, and the rainbow sparkles returned.

The next minute, Billy saw his exercise book. The fizzy feeling was still with him and he felt it travel to his head. And when it got there, the fizzes popped like those lights going on. Then they went through his arm to his hand.

He bent his head, and began writing. And like before, once he started one word, another came to him. It was as though those lights were flowing through his fingers to his pen on to the paper.

He was so busy writing his story he didn't realise that the half hour had gone until he heard, "Did you match them all correctly?"

Miss Murray stood there, tapping what she had in her hand.

Billy put his pen down. What a shame. He had enjoyed writing that story. He hoped Miss Murray would choose him to read out. Another idea came to him.

He shuffled his feet under the table and tapped his fingers on the book, waiting for his table's turn. The rhythm of his tapping matched his thumping heart.

He didn't know if Miss Murray had heard him making noises or not, but when she got to their table she said, "Billy. I saw you writing away. Do you have your answers?"

"I do, miss," he almost shouted out.

"OK, then. Give us your answers," she said, watching him.

"I put them into a story, miss."

"Oh, that's a good idea," she replied, winking at him. He noticed she had that excited look in her eye again. The wink put him off for a minute. He just stood there. What could it mean?

Billy took a deep breath, then read out loud, "Bobby the budgie was fed up stuck in his cage. He could see the beauty of outdoors. Then his owner opened his cage door. When she wasn't looking, Bobby took the chance, and flew out. Now he could fly home to see his friends in Australia. Bobby flew and flew." He flapped his arms up and down as though he was flying away. "On his journey home, Bobby passed many other countries. His first sight of a different animal was when he gazed down at a huge amount of yellow, and on this

yellow he saw animals with humps;

camels." Billy stopped. He walked round

his desk, and, bending over with his hand

over his back, he lolloped like a camel.

Then he wiggled his mouth around and

spat. When he finished, he went back to

his desk – to see a few others had copied

him. A few were spitting and wiggling

their mouths, others were lolloping

about, flapping their hands around like a

hump.

Miss Murray was smiling. That smile spurred him on.

He continued. "Bobby flew further down the country then, and here he kept high in the sky, as he saw lions," and he roared like one, "prowling around the desert area, looking for food. He'd keep away from them. He certainly didn't want to get near those fierce teeth. He also spotted antelopes with their horns sticking up, not far from where the lions were. They were sipping water from a small puddle. He stayed high. He didn't want to get pronged by those sharp horns. Then he passed China, where he spotted the amazing sight of black and white pandas amidst bushes, chewing bamboo." Billy moved his mouth up and down as though he was chewing bamboo, and he picked up a pencil from his desk and mimed chewing it. Out of the corner of his eye, he saw the others copying him again. He grinned.

"Bobby was getting tired from his journey. Finally he reached his home country. He rested on a tree branch, and met Kim the koala, with her sticky-out grey eyes and bobbly tail. Bobby flew and flew until he saw another blue bird that looked liked him. At last, here was home. And he sat on a tree. Tired, but happy."

Billy then yawned himself, as he, too, was tired, like his budgie. He put his book on the table.

Miss Murray laughed.

Then the class copied Billy one last time – they put their heads on their desks and snored, faking sleep.

Miss Murray clapped. "OK, everyone. Stay awake! Billy, you've done it again. You've made a story from it all. I like it. I think you might have found your thing. But I'm not sure that the spitting was needed. Take note, class. That is true storytelling."

They all raised their heads, looking at Billy.

His socks tickled him then, so much so that Billy was tempted to bend down and scratch his leg. He even lowered his hand to reach the itch. But the bell rang then.

Miss Murray called out, "Collect your rewards, and that includes you, Billy."

Billy got a silver star for his work. And another smile, like the ones his mum did.

At the end of the day, his mum came to collect him at the school gates.

"Had a good day, Billy?" she asked, holding out her hand to him.

"Not bad," he mumbled. "I got a silver star in literacy for a good story and a silver star in geography for another story I wrote from a quiz."

"Oh, Billy. You are doing well. You must be doing something right."

Yes, but what was it? And how did he do it?

At six pm Billy sat concentrating on the TV. After today's lessons, where he was praised, he wanted to take note of how the professional presenters did their job.

The News came on.

"Oh," he said, smiling, "George Alagiah is back."

Casper snorted.

His mum said, "Casper. Quiet."

In his bedroom later, Billy got out his list. He gave geography a tick. First literacy, now geography. Both had words in. Was that his thing? Did he need to concentrate on words and pictures?

Chapter Six

Over dinner, Casper told their mum and dad, "I heard today that Billy got only one of his sums right and his cookies tasted horrible."

"Billy, is that true?" his mum asked, though her voice was kind.

He nodded.

"Oh, Billy. No wonder you're quiet. Ah, but Casper," she then said, "Billy has told me that he got two silver stars as well." She drew on the paper in the centre of the table: an upside-down smile, which she changed to a smile. He drew a tick against it.

"I got one pen and two gold stars," Casper said.

Great, Billy thought, Casper always had to go one step ahead of him in everything.

Billy saw his mum wink at his dad then. *What was that about?* He looked at his mum, then his dad. He was sure both had that twinkle of excitement in their eyes. Just like Miss Murray.

Then his mum turned to him and winked. What was she doing? Had she got a plan to help him? Did it involve Miss Murray?

That night, as Billy watched his mum get his clothes out and put them on his chair, he rolled over to hear if she said anything to them.

If she did, it had to be a whisper because he didn't hear a thing.

"Goodnight, Billy. Well done today."

She gave him a thumbs-up..

"Night, Mum," he said.

He watched her leave his room, close the door behind her, waiting until he heard her go downstairs. As soon as he heard the click of the door, Billy climbed out of bed. He picked up his torch and shone it towards his chair.

He looked through his clothes, especially the socks on top. They looked normal. The boring grey ones to go with his uniform. And they looked the same size and shape. Turning his torch off, he climbed back into bed.

He looked back at his clothes and blinked. He was sure there was a glow to them that he hadn't seen just a minute ago. A glow like the moon reflecting on to them. And they were showing all the colours of the rainbow. Strange: it was either his imagination as the moon was white and you couldn't see rainbows at night, or the hall light shining on them.

He rolled back over, closing his eyes.

Chapter Seven

The next morning, Billy rose with a bounce in his step. He remembered the day before and what he had done at school, and the glow of the socks. With this in mind, he got washed and dressed in record time.

As Billy walked into the playground he was sure he felt a slight tickle down on his ankle. *Was it because he was at school, where he could do well, that his socks behaved strangely?*

His first lesson was literacy.

Now, he had done very well yesterday, and had really enjoyed writing what he did. He stepped into the classroom looking forward to the lesson.

Miss Murray said, "Okay, class, I want you to write a story about the sentence on the board." She pointed to what she had written.

Billy looked at the board, and read: "You are in a sports team and have one chance to help them win."

"You can choose what sport you want. You have thirty minutes. Starting now," she said, pressing that watch again.

Billy bent his head. He loved football, so he'd write about that. This was something he could write lots about, he thought, his heart beating in excitement.

His pen heard his thoughts as it shone silver, then the colours of the rainbow. He was about to visit the mysterious world again. This time it was all about sports, so what would he be like now? Time to find out, Billy realised, as he felt his body go light.

Now used to the sensation, he waited until the colours around him stopped sparkling before he opened his eyes. Once the sparkling was over, Billy felt the fizziness in his mouth.

When he opened his eyes he was in front of the screen, which was showing a football match. Up above the pitch, he saw the presenters. Wow! One of them looked like Gary Lineker. And looking closer, Billy saw it wasn't just any match, but a school football match, and there, in clear focus, was him with the football.

Remembering before, Billy ran about, pretending he was playing football. As he did, he called, "And Billy has the ball again. Will he be able to get past the other team?"

The scene faded and the rainbow sparkles appeared.

When he felt a pen in his hand, the fizzy feeling travelled from his mouth through to his arm, then hand. He also felt it in his feet. Ah. It was about football, so he had to show himself playing it like he had to the watching children.

He began writing and, just like before, as an idea came to him, he couldn't stop. He was still writing when Miss Murray said, "Time's up. Billy. I said stop."

He looked up, and said, "Sorry," bowing his head.

One by one, one boy, then one girl was asked to tell their story, until she got to him.

"As you were writing so much, I hope you have something good to tell us, Billy." She had that twinkle in her eye once more.

"Can I stand up to tell it, miss?" he asked.

"Sure. Go ahead."

He waited for a comment from Alistair, but when none came, he stood up, with his paper in his hand.

He pictured himself as the TV presenter, took a deep breath, then said, "I am in my football team and we have to win by one goal. It is up to me and ..." The presenter in him took over. "And there goes Billy Bottomsby with the ball. Can he outrun the other team?" He ran on the spot as though he was running with the ball.

"And number six of the other side is on his tail. What will he do?" Billy pretended to kick a ball to someone else. Then back to him. "And Billy has the ball again. He can hear the crowd roar his name. He can hear the thudding of the players running after him. He's near the goalie. He's in line. Can he get it in?" By this time, Billy was bouncing up and down as though he was the excited presenter. He came to a stop. "And that's when you told us to finish."

The room was silent. Oh no. They all thought it was terrible. But then the room filled with laughter. First there were titters, then they soon turned into snorts, and full laughs.

He gazed up and around him. All his class were laughing. And not at him, for once. Even Miss Murray was chuckling.

"Oh, Billy. That was fantastic. Well done. You get a silver star," she said, giving him a thumbs-up sign.

It wasn't the idea of getting another silver star that pleased Billy, but the sight of Alistair chuckling at his story. He'd won that bet; all he had to do was win the other one.

At lunch time, Billy was asked by Charlie Nimble, "How did you get so good at telling stories?"

"I don't know. I've always liked the lesson, so maybe the sort of exercises that come up have sparked ideas in me," he replied, tilting his head.

"Whatever. You're so funny when you tell them," Charlie said.

"Thanks," Billy replied with a smile.

He felt so happy inside, like the sun shining in him at the warm and kind words from Charlie, instead of the usual teasing and being called Boring Billy.

Then he shook his head in disbelief. It wasn't the feeling of being happy that made him do so but the sparkling rainbow he saw appear above Charlie when he'd told him he was funny.

"What's up, Billy?" Charlie asked, staring at him. "You look like you've seen a ghost."

"Nothing," he replied, shaking his head. What did it all mean? First Alistair and now Charlie. Were they both going to be shown something like he had been?

When he thought that, his socks tickled him. He frowned. *Had it anything to do with them that he could tell a great story? Was it them that made him visit the magical world?* And that got him thinking more.

Chapter Eight

It was music next.

His socks didn't tickle him as he walked into the classroom. He wasn't that good at music, always being out of tune or playing his instrument late in turn. Could he get better at it today? He'd give it a go.

But it was singing today. He did his best to keep in tune, but he saw his teacher look at him and shake her head. She then put her hands over her ears. Oh no, he wasn't that bad, was he?

No, he wasn't good at this kind of art.

Next was science.

Could he be good at making things? He couldn't bake, so could he make things? He'd do his best.

"Okay. Today we are going to make kites, then take them out to the grounds to see how high they can fly and do a quiz as to why you think they fly or not," Miss Murray said. "I want you to split into pairs."

Charlie joined him. "I'll be your kite buddy," he said.

"Great," Billy said, beaming at his new friend.

They followed the instructions on the table, but when it came to trying the kite out in the playground and Billy ran forward with it, he heard a thunk behind him. He turned round to see the kite on the ground. It was a failure.

"You try, Charlie," Billy said, his shoulders drooping.

So Charlie took the kite and ran with it. Billy watched. Charlie dropped the kite on to the ground with a thud.

"Sorry, Billy. It was too big to hold," Charlie told him, sighing.

Billy looked at all the others; a few were just off the ground, others were in the air.

After another ten minutes, Miss Murray called to them. "Lower your kites and bring them back to the classroom. We'll go through the quiz." She started walking back into the building. Billy trudged to the room, behind Charlie.

Charlie went back to his own seat, and Billy plopped into his.

Billy felt his heart beat loud like a drumbeat getting louder and louder as Miss Murray got nearer to his table. And as she did, his stomach dropped lower inside him; he was dreading how the rest of the class would react to his story.

"Billy? You were with Charlie. He hasn't said anything about your kite," Miss Murray said.

Billy slowly raised his head.

He mumbled, "It didn't fly, miss."

There were titters at his table. They had heard him. He glanced Alistair's way. Wow! Alistair was silent for once.

"Oh, Billy. What a shame. You'll find out what you're good at, I know," Miss Murray told him.

Billy looked at her. She had said something like that before. How did she know about his wish?

Miss Murray said, "Next lesson we will go through all the reasons why a kite can fly and reasons it can't."

The bell rang then, saving Billy from the teasing of the others, because he ran out of the room. As he ran, Miss Murray's words about finding out what he was good at rang in his head. He would find out. He wasn't any good at making or baking things, so he knew now he wasn't creative that way. He crossed music and science out. But then he had been good at telling stories and acting them out. *Was that it?* His socked tickled him. *Maybe they were telling him it was.*

Chapter Nine

His mum was at the gate.

"How was your day, Billy?" she asked.

"Good," he replied.

"Really? Tell me about it on the way home."

And he did. He talked, fast, about the good lessons, leaving out the failures.

"That's great, Billy. I am so pleased. What about the rest of your day?" she asked, walking towards the gate.

"I flopped at making a kite, and I can't sing a note," he mumbled.

"Never mind, Billy. You'll work out what you can do." She held the gate open for him.

Billy shook his head. Those were the words that Miss Murray had said. Strange that both his mum and his teacher knew about his wish.

Just before they went into the house, his mum asked, "How were the socks?"

"Not that bad." He wanted to tell his mum about them and what he had thought, but didn't know if she would believe him.

"Good. Pleased to hear it," she said, winking at him. Was it him? Or did his mum's eyes have an extra sparkle when she mentioned the socks? Did she know about them? That wink meant something, he knew, but didn't know what.

Over dinner, Casper said, rolling his eyes, "I heard that you had your literacy class doubled over in laughter. I told them not to be stupid, our Billy didn't do that. Did you?"

Billy smiled. "Yes, I did."

"You're joking!" Casper exclaimed, his mouth going into an O.

"No, I'm not," Billy said.

"Mum, tell Billy he's joking," Casper said, pointing at him.

"Billy's right," she said.

"How?" Casper asked, eyes wide in disbelief.

"I don't know. The answers and words just came to me," Billy said. Then he drew a wink on the paper.

Their mum smiled at him. She knew something was going on.

He watched his mum closely from his bed that night as she took his clean clothes out.

As soon as he heard her start muttering, he turned his head to the side, trying to hear what she was saying, but she was too quiet. He'd have to wait for the morning to see what happened.

"Goodnight, Billy," she said, kissing his cheek.

"Night, Mum," he said.

He watched her put the clothes on his chair, then leave the room.

He kept his eye on the door, until he heard her go down the stairs. Then he rolled over and looked at his clothes. He frowned.

Was it him? Or did he see the top of the pile of clothes glow in the dark? No, the light was shining on them, was all.

He closed his eyes.

The last thought that came to him before darkness came was, *I will show you, Casper, and everyone, what I can do. You wait until tomorrow.*

Chapter Ten

It was now Thursday.

Billy bounced out of bed, stopping by his chair with the clothes on.

He stared at the socks on top, remembering the light he'd seen the night before. He picked them up. Yes, he thought, one looks darker than the other. Strange socks. If they didn't match, would they act the same? He had to wait and see. Walking into the kitchen to have his cornflakes, he said, "Morning, Mum."

"Good morning, Billy," she replied, putting a bowl on the table. "You're in a good mood today."

"Yes. I feel happy. I feel that I can be good at a lesson today," he replied, winking at his mum.

She smiled at him, winking back.

After he'd finished his breakfast, Billy jumped out of his chair and skipped to the sofa to get his schoolbag.

Casper said, "What's got you so cheery today?"

"I'm going to be good at a lesson today," Billy said.

"Oh yes. Who says? Not me." Casper stood, hands on his hips.

"I have a feeling I will be." Billy copied Casper, putting his hands on his hips.

"I have a feeling you won't," Casper said, and sniggered.

You wait and see, Billy thought.

When Billy and his mum got to the school, the socks tickled him like before.

That feeling of doing well just got better, as the tingling sensation floated up his legs and into his body, where he now felt full of energy.

"Have a good day, Billy. Do your best," his mum said, leaving him at the gate.

"Bye, Mum. I will!" he replied, waving to her.

He just knew that he would do well.

Chapter Eleven

Literacy was his second lesson. He had made everyone laugh, so he could be good at this lesson. He would do his best to try again.

Placing paper on a table, Miss Murray said, "There are three pictures on your table. One of a cat, of a car and a child, which could be you. I want you to make a story from those pictures. You have thirty minutes to write it. Good luck."

Billy thought about his neighbour's cat, a black fluffy thing with a huge tail called Kitty, then pictured his road and a car. He bent his head and put pen to paper.

As soon as Billy placed his pen on his exercise book, he waited. Yep. His body was feeling as light as a feather again. And his pen was shining silver, turning into a rainbow. What would he present today? Mmm ... he wondered. He had to write about a cat, car and a boy: that could be himself.

He let the images sparkle around him as he closed his eyes, going with the flow of it.

He opened his eyes when he felt his body go heavy. When he did, he gasped. Wow! In front of him were huge signs. Signs that he'd seen on roads when his mum had taken him and Casper shopping. Was he going to talk about roads?

As he walked towards the children, the fizziness returned. It felt like someone was turning lights on all around inside his head. And with each one, he got more excited at what he could do. He could feel the energy bubbling inside him, eager to show everyone.

When he faced the children, Billy felt

something tug his body. He looked down

and saw that he now wore a bright

yellow jacket. Then a stick, which he

recognised as a lollipop, appeared in his

hand. Ah. He was going to talk about

road safety.

The screen behind him shot into focus.
Billy blinked. Eh? What he saw was ... his
road, and there on one side was him, on
the other, about to walk into the road,
was his neighbour's cat. That was
strange. He'd been thinking about Kitty
before he'd started writing.

Billy knew what the story would be.

"Boys and girls. You can see Billy. He
wants to cross the road to get to the cat.
What should he do first?" he asked the
children.

There was silence.

"Yes, you've guessed it. He needs to look one way for traffic, then the other and then the first way again." He showed the children how by looking left, then right, and left again.

Then he heard a car coming. He had an idea for the story, and how he could act it out. As soon as he thought that, the air around him began to sparkle rainbow colours, and Billy went with the feeling again.

Back to seeing a whiteboard, he picked up his pen and felt the light warm through him from his head to his arm and his hand, until the tips of his fingers felt like they were tingling with energy. He started writing, and pictures like a film came to him. He wrote and wrote.

He stopped now and then, tapping his pen on his table. Then another picture came to him. He sighed and carried on writing.

His name being said loudly brought Billy out of his thoughts.

Everyone was looking at him.

"Billy, I said time's up," Miss Murray said, glancing at the clock on the wall.

"Oh. Sorry, miss." He put his pen down.

"It's okay, Billy. Seeing as you were busy in your work, I'll let you go first and read your story to us."

Billy beamed.

"Thanks, miss," he said, standing up.

Miss Murray winked at him. And he noticed her eyes had that extra sparkle like his mum's had when she'd mentioned the socks.

Encouraged by this, he thought, *She must know I'll be all right.*

He stood up, took a deep breath and began reading. "I stepped out of my gate and heard a meow. I looked to the road and saw Kitty, the cat next door. I was going to walk on, when I heard the noise of a car coming. 'Mum,' I said, 'Kitty is in the road and could be run over.' 'Stay where you are. I'll see if I can get to her,' Mum said. Then I heard it. The car was getting faster. It needed someone faster than it to get there before my mum. It called for Super Billy." He raised his arms, pretending he was going to fly.

"Then everything around me got clearer. As I watched for traffic, a breeze touched my face. Out of the corner of my eye, I saw an empty crisp bag on the ground. Ignoring this, I dropped my schoolbag on to the ground. At the road, I looked left, then right and left again," and he looked one way, then another and back again to show the class what to do. "The car wasn't that near Kitty. I could get to her in time." He copied what the presenter had done, and made it appear that he was stepping into the road. "All I wanted to do was save Kitty. I picked up Kitty, and dashed to the other side of the road." He pumped his arms up and down to show running.

"As I stepped on to the other side, the car sped by. Phew! Just in time." He wiped his brow with his hand as though wiping sweat away.

"'You all right, Kitty?' I asked the cat. 'Meow,' she called. Then, ow! She had clawed my hand. I dropped her then." He pretended to stroke a cat, then flung his arms wide like he'd been scratched and had dropped the cat. "Where had Kitty gone? Back across the road and into the arms of her owner.

"I followed her over. 'Billy,' my neighbour said with a huge smile. 'I saw what you did for Kitty. I'm so grateful you saved her. Thank you. Come to me after school and I'll have a treat as a reward.' When my neighbour had gone into her house, Mum said, "That was a silly but brave thing to do. Well done.'

"'Let's get to school,' Mum said," Billy finished. "And that's where I had to stop cos I had run out of time to write more."

He put down his book, looking around him at his classmates.

There were smiles, and others were
nodding. Then someone burst out
laughing. Billy shook his head with
surprise; it was Miss Murray herself who
was laughing.

"Oh, Billy. That was brilliant. You have a way with you when you tell a story. What do you think, class?" she asked, turning towards the rest of the room. The faces all smiled; then came the laughter. The loudest, he noticed, was coming from Alistair, sounding like a ship's horn blaring. He hoped there was no more teasing from him, but laughter from now on.

"Billy, I think you could be a great TV presenter or storyteller one day if you tried." Miss Murray gave him a thumbs-up.

Billy thought about this. *Yes, miss was right. He felt that this was the one thing that he could be really good at. And he would be.*

Then he realised what Miss Murray had said. How did she know about the TV presenter?

"Billy. You get two gold stars and a pen for making me laugh. Well done."

As she walked past him, Billy saw her wink at him. *What was that for?*

As he wondered, his socks tickled him to say, "You get it now."

Oh yes. He got what he had to do. And he'd try again.

Walking back to her desk, Miss Murray called out, "Collect your stars on the way out, please."

Billy joined the queue.

When Miss Murray had stuck the two gold stars into his book, she then gave him a pen and drew a big smile on his page. She said, wiggling an eyebrow at him, "Well done again, Billy. Watch out for that cat, though."

He left the room frowning. *What did that mean? It was only a story, wasn't it?*

Chapter Twelve

The good feeling was still there at lunchtime as he was standing against a wall in the playground, when the football team said, "Play with us, Billy." He felt his heart beat loud with excitement, not dread, at the thought of being in a team.

Billy said, "Okay," joining another boy he knew from his class.

It was half way through the game when Billy realised something – the scene he was seeing was the one from his story. One of the other team was coming towards him with the ball. He could feel his heart beating like a drum. It was pounding louder and louder, until the other boy got so close to him and he could hear it making a tap-tap sound like the ball bouncing up and down on the ground.

This was it. This was the moment. He ran to the other boy and kicked the ball away from him, then he caught up with the ball. He took it away from the other team, and went this way and that way, running round all the others, until he was facing the goal.

Now was the point that he became a hero and scored. He felt his socks tickle him then and smiled. *Okay, he told them. I can do it. I know I can.* And he kicked the ball on and on and on until ... it went into the goal, past the goalkeeper's hands.

Cheers of "Hurray for Billy! Hurray for Billy!" sounded all around, and he was lifted off the ground by his team-mates.

Then a deep voice calling out, "Put him down. You could hurt him," made them put Billy back down.

They all stood there as the Headmaster, Mr Bloomer, came towards them.

"That was a good goal, Billy. Well done," Mr Bloomer boomed.

Billy blinked. The Head was telling him he had been great.

"Thank you, sir," he said.

Mr Bloomer smiled, waving him away.

Billy blinked even more. The Head smiling didn't happen that often. He had to be great now.

Chapter Thirteen

And Miss Murray, in ICT, thought so, too.

Drawing a smiley face on the board, Miss Murray said, "I want each table to do a presentation about feeling good. The best one will get a pen."

Billy knew just the thing to do, as he was feeling good about himself. So when the others at his table asked, "Anyone have any ideas?" he said, "I do."

"It can be about me. At the start of the week I was boring and sad. Now I've found what I'm good at and am happy and make people laugh with me, so I'm not boring any more. It's made me feel good about myself." He felt his heart beat at what the others might think about his idea.

"Excellent," Charlie said. He had asked to join them in place of one of the girls. "Okay. Let's say you're in charge of the idea and presentation, Billy," he said.

The others looked at him, nodding.

Billy beamed at them. For the first time,

he felt accepted by others, not ridiculed.

"You are good at telling a story, Billy,"

Charlie said, chortling. "You've had us all

in stitches."

Charlie offered to help paint the poster after the girls had done the outline. Billy told them his idea, and one of the others drew it, whilst another wrote the words. When the poster was finished and they showed Billy, he said, "That's good. What I had in mind to do." He could tell they were all pleased.

"Are you finished yet? I'll give you five more minutes before we start the presentations," Miss Murray said.

This time Billy's heart was beating with excitement, not dread. He knew that presenting a story was one of the things he was good at, so hoped that he wouldn't let his team down. His socks tickled him. It felt like the ants were jumping up and down with joy. *Ah*, he thought. *They knew he'd be good at this.*

When Miss Murray reached their table, she said, "Who is going to do the presentation?"

"Me," Billy said, standing up.

"I should've guessed! Go on, Billy, tell us your story of feeling good." Her eyes were sparkling again. He'd come to realise it meant his teacher had faith in him.

Out of the corner of his eye, Billy saw the rest of the class sit up and lean forwards. They were expecting things from him. *Okay then*, he thought, *you'll get it!*

"This is a story about me and how I felt good," he told the class. "At the start of the week, I was boring and fed up with my brother always bragging about how clever he was at school. So I decided I would be, too." Billy didn't mention the socks; he didn't think anyone would believe him. Even he wasn't that sure about them. "As the week went by, I found out I was good at telling stories and acting them out, but not good at things like making kites." He drew a sad face on a piece of paper as though he was feeling bad about that and held it up.

There were a few titters.

"But ... I still wanted to be good at something. What did I do? I focussed on the lessons I had guessed I was good at, and where I could tell stories: English, geography, and any that I could make stories from by matching people and pictures. Day by day, I got better and better, and got rewarded for them." He held up a gold star, then a pen.

"And to top it all, I made my class, including my teacher, laugh, not at me, but with me. For someone who had been boring and average at the start of the week, this was a boost." He beamed at his class to show how happy he was. "And for once I feel happy. I know what I can be good at, and will continue to be good at. I am a happier person now, not a fed-up one." As he said this, one of his team held up a picture of a smiling boy. "Me!" he said.

"So my motto is, to find out what makes you happy and what you can be good at and work on that. Only then will you be happy with who you are." And it dawned on him then that that was what he had come to do – accept who he was and what he could do with his disability.

He stopped talking.

After a minute, the room filled with clapping and cheering.

When it had quietened down, Miss Murray said, "Now that was a brilliant story about how to feel good. I believe that everyone can learn from that. Well done, Billy. For that excellent presentation, you get your stationery set of a pen, pencil and rubber."

"Now that makes me happy," Billy said.

Everyone laughed. He gazed round the room. But then he saw both Charlie and Alistair frowning. What were they thinking? About what they could be good at? He started to wonder, too.

At the end of the lesson, when he collected his stars, Miss Murray said, "Well thought-out presentation, Billy. I am glad you have now worked out what you can do. Keep up the good stories. I'm looking forward to hearing more from you." She drew a huge smile on his page.

"Thanks, miss," he said, and walked

out of the room, his head held high.

Chapter Fourteen

Billy took his own advice in the history lesson.

Miss Murray said, "I know you've had enough of tests this week, but this is the last one. I want you to match the names of the people to the pictures of the places they are known for, but with a difference. I want you all to take a leaf out of Billy's book and see if you can make a story from the pictures. You have thirty minutes. Don't forget, Billy is your role model. Let's see if you can write stories as good as his. Good luck."

When she said the last two words, Miss Murray winked at him.

Billy smiled. She had given him a challenge.

How could he do what he had done before, and make it better? He thought about what he had done in geography. *Would it work another time? I was good then, and I can be again*, he thought. His socks tickled him, like ants doing a tap dance. *They must think so, too*, he thought.

He looked at the pictures. He went to write, then remembered what had happened before. He waited.

This time it was special. The sparkles shone brighter and the rainbow seemed clearer and glowed like it twinkled in the sky. Was this the last time he'd be seeing himself as a TV presenter? If so, he couldn't wait to see what he did, knowing it was history.

Billy didn't close his eyes. He wanted to experience it all properly.

As he flew through the tunnel of sparkles, he twirled round and round, giddy with the sensation. He was glad when he came to a stop, and in front of him was the TV studio once more.

As soon as he was standing still, the fizzing returned. It was stronger this time, like he had sweets popping everywhere in his mouth and they wouldn't stop.

When he got nearer, Billy saw that on the walls behind his seat were pictures of people. He recognised a few of them as part of history. He wondered who he'd be talking about today.

He faced the camera. "Good morning, boys and girls. Today we are going back in time as it's our history lesson. We will be walking through the decades. First we'll visit the 20th century to visit one special lady. She was the first woman to fly over the Atlantic. Yes, we are about to meet Amelia Earhart." The screen showed a lady standing next to a small airplane. As the screen came into focus, Billy saw that she was wearing a brown suit and had short dark hair. Amelia Earhart.

"Here comes Billy to fly with Amelia!" Billy opened his arms out wide and began to walk around the studio making noises, "Eeooww!" Just like a plane. Okay, that's what he had to do to make the story come alive. And he knew what he'd call himself: Billy, The Time Explorer.

Who would he visit next, and in which century?

He watched Amelia and himself fly off in the plane. As the plane prepared to land, Billy bent down to the floor, closing his arms against his body.

He looked up at the screen again.

He appeared to be on a TV set. He recognised camera teams from before and glanced around.

The camera focussed on one man, who had bright green hair. He watched and listened to him, sure there was a reason why he was there.

The man said to the camera, "Hello, I'm Alan Gardner, the Autistic Gardener."

Autistic? Billy thought. He was, too. He now watched him more closely, and saw that, yes, he, the gardener, was like him. He couldn't look people in the eye.

As Billy continued watching Mr Gardner, he thought, if he has autism like me and can present his own TV show, then maybe I can, too. I want to be like him.

Thank you showing me this, socks, he silently told them.

He was back in the plane with Amelia. She had heard him talk to his socks, and said, "Let's go further into history."

Billy knew what he had to do to win that challenge. He was ready to go back to school. His socks heard him. A rainbow appeared, then the different coloured sparkles shone around him. His body went light as the air that Amelia had flown through.

Knowing it could be the last time he would do this, Billy relaxed as he went round and round. When the spinning stopped his desk was in front of him, his book open, ready for him to write in it.

Now to put what he'd seen into practice.

Billy bent his head to write his story. And what a brilliant story it would be! With this thought, the popping stayed in his mouth, and travelled all through his body until he felt like the whole of him alight with warmth and excitement. He wiggled his fingers; they felt restless with tingling energy. He was ready to write.

Like before, the pictures came to him like a film rolling in his mind. As the film went on, Billy wrote. He recalled himself as the explorer who had gone back in time.

He wrote and wrote and wrote.

This time, he did hear Miss Murray call out, "Time's up. Put down your pens, please."

He did, happy with his story.

He listened to all the others tell their stories, and boy, had they taken Miss Murray up on her challenge. There was the history buff with an essay on the characters and places; a drama enthusiast who had written a play with all the characters, and the traveller who pretended to travel with them.

He thought that some were good, even very good, but they weren't that imaginative, and didn't act out the scenes like he did to bring the story to life. When he thought this, Billy realised then what made his stories special – he made them come alive with his actions, just like he had in the magical world, and like Michael Palin did. It was thanks to the mysterious world that he had visited.

When Miss Murray reached his table, he listened to one of the others talk, shuffling his feet with impatience. He knew that Miss Murray would ask him to read, and he was excited at the prospect.

"Billy, what delights have you got for us today?" Miss Murray asked, beaming at him.

"I am Billy, the time explorer," he said, standing up.

"Ah, this sounds exciting. Go ahead, Billy, the time explorer."

Seeing Miss Murray's sparkly eyes, he continued, knowing she was excited about what he could do.

"I was writing about Amelia Earhart in history, when suddenly the air around me turned into a cloud. I blinked. When I opened my eyes, I jumped. There in front of me was Amelia herself, by her plane. 'Hello, Billy,' she said. 'Come and fly with me.' 'Okay,' I replied, and I followed her into the plane. I strapped myself in, and felt my body go light when the plane took off and went up into the sky. From up above, the trees were small, like branches. I was watching the scenery, when it turned into a cloud again. We flew through the clouds," and he spread

his arms out like wings and went

'eeooww', like a plane.

"Up, up we flew." Billy acted as though

he was going up, stretching himself on to

his toes to make it look like he was taking

off.

"And on and on we went, until we

landed in the filming of a TV garden

show. I watched the presenter, Alan

Gardner, and realised why we had

landed there. Let me show you. Charlie,"

he said.

Charlie looked at Billy, and Billy turned away as though he wasn't keeping eye contact with him.

"Alan Gardner calls himself the Autistic Gardener. So, if he can become a garden presenter with autism, then so can I become a presenter."

Back at his desk, Billy continued. "Amelia agreed. We came to another cloud. We went from a busy and noisy TV show to ... the peace of hills. And as we got closer to the green, I saw a man walking around. I heard him say, 'I wander as lonely as a cloud.'" Billy walked round his desk, his finger to his mouth as though he was thinking, then muttering the words.

"That line rang a bell with me. I'd heard it before, but where? It wasn't until we got within a few feet from him that I realised who he was and why I'd heard those words before. We were watching Wordsworth writing his famous poem, one that I'd heard Casper, my brother, learn for his homework recently. So we had to be in the 19th century and in the Lakes, where Wordsworth lived. Amelia and I stayed here for the a while, getting our calm lives back to normal." He held his arms out at the sides, stretching on to his toes.

"Then she flew us up and away again.
Wordsworth was good for the English
language, she said. ' I think what you've
seen today has tired you out, so I'm
taking you for a rest, where the lady I
know will look after you well.' Amelia
flew up and away again. I shook my
head. It was hard to take in all that I'd
seen. I certainly was a time explorer.
From one century to another.

"As the plane went through another cloud, we entered a scene of chaos, of men limping and bleeding, all walking towards a building." Here, Billy created the scene, limping around his desk and holding an arm to his body like it had been hurt. "The scenes inside the building came clearer to me then, and I saw one lady in a black and white dress, wearing a black hat and carrying a lamp. The name 'Lady with the Lamp' came to mind, and I knew who she was. Florence Nightingale. 'She's ... ' I said. 'I know.'

Amelia said, 'Tell her Amelia sent you to have a rest.' We landed not far from the hospital." Billy crouched down to make it look like he was landing the plane.

"When Amelia took off, I walked to the building." Here Billy made a shuffling walk as though he was tired and needed a rest. "I was expected as Florence Nightingale met me at the door. 'Come in, Billy,' she said. 'I understand that you need a rest after a long trip with Amelia. I have a bed for you.' She led me to a bed in a corner. 'Have a good rest,' she said. I lay down in the bed and closed my eyes.

"When I heard my name being called, I opened them to find I was back in the classroom. I had fallen asleep and had my head in my arms." Billy returned to his seat and sat down. He then put his head on his arms and snored for effect. "Wow, I am exhausted after that long plane journey," he said.

Everyone laughed, including Miss Murray, her eyes twinkling.

She said, "Well, after listening to you all, I have to say, sorry, but no one can match our Billy and his action stories. Billy, you win. You get five gold stars for that. Well done."

Billy glanced at Charlie and Alistair. Both were clapping hard for him, and both had clear sparkling rainbows like his as they clapped.

His socks and the magical world had come to his rescue again. But he now knew what he could do and how to do it, and he would do more. Oh yes. He was on his way to winning that bet with Casper.

Chapter Fifteen

The bell rang then.

After collecting his rewards, he skipped out to where his mum was standing at the front gate.

"Hello, Billy. Looks like you had a good day," she said, smiling at him.

"I did. I scored for the team at lunch, and got gold stars in literacy. I made Miss Murray laugh with my story. And I got five gold stars in history for winning a challenge for the best story," he said, jigging up and down.

"Oh, Billy, that's wonderful," his mum said.

Wait until he told Casper. He couldn't wait to see his brother's reactions.

He didn't have to wait long, because Casper got home ten minutes after they did.

And the first thing he said was, "Hey, Billy. You never guess what I heard today."

Billy raised his eyebrows.

"I heard that you made your class and teacher laugh in literacy, and you won a history challenge. Now that made me laugh." Casper put his arms to his tummy, making out he was laughing.

"You heard right, Casper," their mum told him.

Billy almost laughed himself, when he saw Casper stop still, then suck his lips. A sign, Billy knew, that he was angry.

"And I got two gold stars for making Miss Murray laugh," Billy added. So there, he told Casper silently.

Casper walked to the dining table, and scraped his chair back, making a screeching noise. Oh dear. He only did that when he was angry with someone, and that someone was him, Billy knew.

After dinner, Casper and Billy sat at the table and did their homework. Billy bent his head and got on with his writing, not taking any notice of Casper. Until he heard a groan of, "This is hard," and Casper sighing.

Billy raised his head.

It looked like Casper was having trouble. Should he help him?

Another groan made his mind up for him. He would, as he knew that if he didn't then he wouldn't hear the end of Casper's moaning.

"Want my help?" he offered, leaning towards Casper.

"No!" Casper shouted, putting his arms round his books.

Billy knew different.

He saw Casper scratch his head, then look up at him.

"Okay, then," he agreed.

"What's the problem?"

"Literacy. It's the end of term quiz and we have to make a story linking the words we've been given. I've managed two out of the eight, and got stuck."

"Let's have a look and see what we can do."

Billy got up and walked round to Casper's side of the table. He picked up the book and read it.

"Oh, I see. You have to have a good imagination."

"I've tried ..."

"I think we have our own talents. You're good at brainy topics like maths and science, and I'm good at imagining things and acting them out. That's what you've got to do. Imagine them as a film or TV programme that you like. Or you could draw them. You can draw really well, better than me. So try that and see what you can come up with. Have a go."

"Thanks, Billy."

"Pleasure."

Billy sat down, watching Casper. He had bent his head over his book and started drawing. Good. He'd gone with the idea.

It took a minute before Billy started his own work because all he could think about was that he'd helped Casper for once. It felt good.

After half an hour, Billy put down his pen; he'd finished. And, so it seemed, had Casper, who put his pen down, too, and smiled.

"Thank you, Billy. That helped. I wonder how I'll get on tomorrow. I might get a reward. One to boost my many this week."

Casper hadn't forgotten the bet, despite his having helped him out, Billy realised.

"And I might win one or two, too," Billy replied.

"May the best brother win," Casper said, holding his hand out.

Thinking, we shall see, Billy touched Casper's hand.

Their mum came in then. She saw

Casper hold his hand out to Billy.

Drawing a smile in the air by Billy, she

said, "Well done, Billy, for winning the

competition. And well done, Casper, for

not moaning and gloating at Billy. I'm

proud of both of you for what you can

do." She ruffled Casper's hair.

That night in bed, his mum told Billy,

"Your dad and I are proud of what you

did today."

"Miss Murray said that I could be a great presenter. I did make everyone laugh, so maybe I'll try to keep doing that."

"You do, Billy. If you work hard and try your best at something, then you will do great things." She kissed him on the cheeks.

"Mum!" he said.

"Just to let you know that no matter how you do, we still care for you. You're my baby boy."

"Goodnight, Mum," Billy said.

"Night, Billy."

All thoughts of strange socks and what his teacher had said to him were forgotten with feeling so good about the day's events.

Chapter Sixteen

Until the next morning.

As Billy and his mum walked down their front path to the gate, Billy thought he heard a meow. What Miss Murray had said to him the day before came back to him, and at the same time, he gazed down at his feet.

He hadn't thought if his socks were odd or not, until now, and he looked. One seemed shorter than the other, but he wasn't sure. They hadn't tickled him.

The meow came again, louder.

Billy recalled his story, and his eyes were drawn to the road.

It couldn't be. Could it? Could his story be about to come real?

There was Kitty, his neighbour's black fluffy cat, sitting on the edge of the road. He could feel the breeze on his face. He heard a slight rustle, and he glanced at the pavement. Yes. There was an empty crisp bag on the ground.

"Hold on, Mum," he said. "Kitty's in the road. I need to make sure she won't get run over."

"I'll do ... " his mum began saying, but Billy walked to the edge of the road to grab the cat. Remembering his story and what he'd seen in the magical world, Billy looked to the left, then right and left again. There was a car up the road, but it was too far away to reach him if he was quick. He crossed the road, reaching the cat on the other side. Just as he picked Kitty up, he heard the car speed by. Billy shivered.

What was going on? First Kitty in the road, then the car speeding past him just as he saved her? The breeze and the crisp bag. All of this was in his story. And what he'd seen in that world. It all seemed so strange. Like he was in a dream, or in his case, a story.

His mum's saying, "Billy, don't do that again. You scared me doing that. It was a silly but brave thing to do." That was in the story, too.

A quivering voice calling, "Kitty, Kitty," made Billy aware he was still holding the cat.

"I think I'd best get Kitty back to her owner," he said and, checking for cars, he crossed back over the road.

"Oh, there she is. I thought I saw her in the road," the old lady said, tottering over to him.

"You did. I got to her before a car came by," he told her.

"You saved her, Billy. Thank you. Come to me after school and I'll give you a treat. Have a good day, young man."

Billy turned round and went back to his mum.

"Let's get to school," she said.

He shivered again. *Those words. The same ones he had written in his story. Strange.*

Chapter Seventeen

When they got to the gates, his mum said,

"Be sure to take care, hero."

Billy went red.

After his mum had left, his mates

asked, "What did she mean by hero?"

Billy told them about saving the cat.

"Hero Billy! Hero Billy!" they all

shouted.

News spread like a fire. When he went

to class, he was clapped by the others

who were already there.

Pointing to the board, Miss Murray said, "I heard about what you did, Billy. Well done. For that, you get a gold star."

Billy beamed.

Still his socks didn't tickle him. He felt good anyway, his heart bursting with the warmth of being liked and from being cheered for his actions.

This feeling good and of being liked continued into literacy, and even seeing that it was a spelling test, the one thing he hated, didn't bother him.

He told himself, *I can do it if I try my best.*

"Today, class, I will be telling you six words, and you must spell them for me in your books. Now, these words have been used this week, so no cheating, please. You have twenty minutes to write them down. Okay, the first word is ...

television."

Okay, Billy thought. What he needed to do was to split the word into bits. So first tel...e...vish...on, and he wrote it in his book. He did the same for the rest of the words.

As he wrote the last word and Miss Murray told them, to stop, Billy thought, I think I did okay.

Miss Murray said, "I shall now write the correct spellings on the board, and we can see how well you did."

Billy watched as she wrote out the words.

He didn't get the first one but he got the rest right. Nine out of ten was very good for him.

He looked at his feet. His socks hadn't tickled him at all during the test. And he was sure one of them was shorter.

"So, how did you score?" Miss Murray asked. "Put your hand up if you got more than half right."

Billy put his hand up in the air. Instead of dread, Billy felt pleased and good with himself.

"Well done, all of you. You get a silver star each."

Billy smiled at her. A silver star wasn't as good as a gold one, but to him it meant that he was better than he was before, when he got no stars, and his socks were normal.

At the end of the test, Miss Murray said, "Well done all of you who got stars. Collect them on your way out."

At the desk, as Billy collected his star, Miss Murray said to him, winking, "I did say to look out for that cat."

Billy left the room chuckling at Miss

Murray's words.

Wait until he told his mum, and

especially Casper.

Chapter Eighteen

When they entered the classroom for PHSE later after lunch and sat down, Miss Murray said, "I was going to give you an exercise about feeling good, but after Billy's heroics today, I have thought of another exercise, to do with safety. Billy, could you come up here, please."

Billy got up out of his chair and joined Miss Murray at the front.

As he passed everyone, he saw them nod at him, and he felt proud, not sick with nerves like he used to.

"Billy, I want you to read the passage in your story from yesterday that you think is about safety."

He said, "I need my book, miss."

"I don't think you do. It was what happened this morning, wasn't it?" she said.

How did she know? Then he recalled what she'd said about the cat. And thinking of the cat, he knew what Miss Murray was talking about.

"I saw the cat across the road. I looked left, right, then left again. There was a car way up the road."

"Thank you, Billy. That was the piece I wanted you to tell us. Now, does anyone know why I wanted him to do that?" Miss Murray asked, glancing round the room.

Billy saw everyone look at each other.

He knew what it was.

Heart beating loud like a drum, he said, "Miss, I know. Can I act it out?"

"Of course, Billy. Everyone, watch what Billy does."

He spoke the first sentence. "I looked left, right and left again for traffic," and moved his head left, right and left again. As he spoke, Billy felt the familiar fizzy feeling return. It was a gentler tingling, not the popping like before. It was reminding him he could do this.

He continued, "I saw a car way up the road, so walked across the road," he walked on the spot, "to get the cat."

"Thank you, Billy," she said, giving him a thumbs-up. "That was excellent. I hope everyone learnt from that because I want you all to write down what safety on the road means to you. And you can write it in points or as a story like Billy's. Or in pictures as it is art next, and I want to continue with the subject."

The bell rang when Billy was still writing his thoughts about safety. He had an idea for a safety poster.

For once he stayed in the room, whilst all his friends went outside. He wanted to work on his idea. Not try to be part of a group. This made him realise that he didn't have to be part of a gang to be someone. He could be himself and still be liked.

When everyone came back into the room, Miss Murray said, "I've put paper, pencils and crayons on each table. Think about what you wrote on safety and then create a great poster."

Billy picked up the pencil in front of him and began drawing.

First he drew a circle, then he looked at himself. He bent his head, licked his lips and carried on drawing. A while later, he raised his head and looked at what he'd drawn. The first bit was done. He then did the same picture twice, but made his eyes look left, then right and left again. Now for the extras. He drew another round, but by the bottom of what he'd already drawn. Then to the side of his picture, a small circle with a bigger circle under it. Then he added blobs and a curly line on it. That was Kitty. Next to that he drew a car.

He thought about it. It needed something else. But what? He remembered what the others had called him and he knew. He needed words to match the pictures.

Above the picture he drew a bubble and wrote 'Meow' in it. He drew another bubble over the second drawings he'd done, and wrote 'Super Billy to the rescue' in that. Above the last drawing, he drew one last bubble. In it, he wrote the word 'hero'. Now it needed colour.

He put down the pencil he had used and picked up a brown crayon. He coloured in his top, then his bottom. Next he took a black crayon and coloured in the second picture. Last, he used a yellow crayon, making the 'hero' yellow.

He'd just finished the yellow when Miss Murray called, "Time's up."

There were taps as everyone put down the crayons they'd been using.

"Let's have a look at all your pictures," Miss Murray said, walking towards the front table.

One by one, each table took it in turn to hold up their drawings and show the class what they'd done.

Then it came to his table. And when he showed his picture, Miss Murray said, "Ah, Billy, I can see what you have done. You have given yourself a medal for playing football and saving the cat. Everyone, what do you think?"

All eyes went to him, and that nervous feeling crept back into his head. Billy began shaking. *What if they all thought it terrible? What if he wasn't good because of his socks, after all?*

Then he heard his football mates say, "Billy's a hero. The medal is a good idea."

"Billy, we can see what you want us to see. You are good at something. Well done," Miss Murray told him.

Billy blinked. *Miss Murray knew he wanted to be good at a lesson? How?* It didn't matter. He had been told that his picture was good, which was all he wanted to hear.

As he went to walk past Miss Murray's desk, she said to him, "Billy, if you wait for a moment, I'll give you your gold star."

So, when it was him and Miss Murray at the front of the class, she stuck a gold star in his art book. She also drew a smile, which nearly filled up the rest of the page. As he went to take his book, she winked at him.

At the door, Alistair stopped him.

Uh-oh, now what?

"Billy, that was great. You're no longer weird in my eyes," he said, friendly.

Billy smiled back at him. Oh yes, He'd won that bet about Alistair. Now all he had to do was work out what Miss Murray's winks meant, and win the bet against Casper.

Chapter Nineteen

When he found his mum at the gates, he said, "Guess what, Mum?"

"What, Billy?"she asked, raising an eyebrow.

"I got a gold and silver star today."

"You did? That's great, Billy. You can be as good as Casper."

And those words from his mum made him smile more. To hear her say he was as good as Casper made his day.

When they got home, and Casper was with them, his mum said at the dining table, "Today is a special day."

"Why? Was Billy even more weird than he usually is?" Casper joked, putting his hand over his mouth, pretending to yawn.

"No, Casper. Billy made me proud. Not only did he save the cat next door, but he got a gold and silver star at school."

So, match that, Billy thought.

Casper opened his mouth and closed it, not saying a word.

Billy laughed.

"Oh dear. Don't know what to say for once, Casper? Never mind."

He saw that their mum's mouth was starting to pucker, and he thought she was going to tell him off for teasing Casper, but no, she smiled and then laughed.

"Not nice being teased, is it, Casper?" she said, ruffling his brother's hair.

Slowly, Casper shook his head. Then he said, "Billy, I'm sorry. And ... well done for today. You'll be better than me one day."

"Well, let's find out if I have been this week. Bring out your rewards, and we'll compare them. I bet I have more, so have won our bet. I've not forgotten."

"You're on," Casper said. He got up and went upstairs to his bedroom.

Whilst Casper was gone, Billy went into the living room, where he had his schoolbag on the sofa. First, he took out all his exercise books from his bag. Then he returned to the dining table and placed them on the table. He opened the books to show the stars he'd been awarded.

Next, he went upstairs to his bedroom. He took out the box he'd kept his other rewards in from his wardrobe, then the three pens he'd won, and returned downstairs to the dining table where Casper was waiting. Billy put his pens with his books.

"Okay. Open your books and put anything else you've won on the table," Billy said.

Watching his brother, he began to count in his head the number of stars he saw. With each book on display, the number went up, but Billy smiled. Not so many as he had, he was sure.

When Casper had finished, Billy said, "You count mine and I'll count yours," even though he'd already done it. He wanted this to be a fair contest.

Billy said, "So, what do you make it for me?"

Casper replied, "Two silver and eleven gold stars, and three pens. That is impressive. What about me?" he asked, pointing at himself, chest out.

"Okay. A good amount, but ... you have five silver and five gold stars, and one pen."

"I won the pen today in literacy, which I have you to thank for. I can see how you got your rewards if you do what you told me to do for my homework. It works. So, I think the number of gold stars and pens you have wins it," Casper said.

Wow! It took a lot for Casper to praise him instead of teasing him.

Billy held out his hand.

Casper shook it, saying, "Well done, Billy. You win the bet. I never thought you would beat me at schoolwork, but you have."

Their mum appeared then.

"Mum, I won the bet with Casper," Billy told her, grinning.

"Well done, Billy," she said. She drew a smile on the paper, then wrote something.

When his mum had moved away from the table, Billy read, 'I knew you could do it and find out what you are good at.' Next to it he saw what looked like a drawing of a pair of socks. Eh? It all had to do with his mum, it had to.

Later that night, as Billy got ready for bed, he looked at his socks.

They hadn't tickled him at all in the day. He was sure one was still shorter than the other. He took a closer look. And saw why. One was shorter because it had fallen down his leg. No wonder it didn't feel strange.

Then it dawned on Billy. Even though his socks hadn't acted strange, he had done amazing things today. He'd saved a cat. He'd got a silver star for literacy, spelling and numeracy and a gold star for art. And how?

He had done all of that because for once he had believed in himself after trying his best. And it had worked.

So he could be good at things: he just had to believe in himself.

And he had got praise from Casper!

Then he thought about his mum and Miss Murray, and all that winking at him. He now realised that they were encouraging him in what he did, and maybe weren't magical after all.

Now he knew what he was good at, he would try and try again. *He could be better. He would be that presenter Miss Murray had said he could be.*

Meanwhile, from the sparkles he'd seen round Charlie and Alistair, it looked like he was needed to help them. He'd helped Casper with his homework and that felt good. So, he could do the same for them. It could help him become more confident and maybe get to be a presenter.

He closed his eyes. He dreamt of himself telling a story, and there in the audience was his mum, smiling, clapping and winking at him.

A message from Julie

Thank you for buying and reading this ebook. If you wish to be one of the first to know when I have a new book out or coming out in print, then why not sign up to my newsletter on the front page of my website. You will get a free short story, which is the prequel to Billy.

Acknowledgements

I would like to thank:

Dr Hilary Johnson for her edits and comments which have made it read as a better book.

Rachel Lawston of Lawston Designs for the cover and illustrations

My fellow members of the Soceity of Children's Book Writers and Illustrators for the information about lessons, how many teachers classes have and vocabulary.

About the author:

I live in SE London. I am an indie author of adult and children's ebooks. Billy is loosely based on what I was like at primary school, when I thought I was just shy and quiet, and didn't want to read out loud in class and found it hard to make friends. The idea for 'Billy' came from me wearing odd socks. I wear socks the same colour and they often get mixed up, so I might wear one lighter or shorter than the other. I thought, what if socks could make a little boy become super at school, but didn't know how or why, and

I didn't know why he needed to be super to others. Then a couple of years ago I got the chance to see the play 'The Curious Incident of the Dog in the Night Time' which has a teenage boy with Asperger's Syndrome in. I knew why my character was boring and needed to be super. Then I got the idea that the socks could take him to a magical world where he saw himself as being confident. The book grew from there, and so did the rest of the series. It wasn't until 2011 when I was diagnosed with Asperger's Syndrome that I knew why I was like I was as a child, and still am as an adult. I blog about my writing life, and my Asperger's Syndrome.

Another message from Julie

Also, if you really liked this book, then please could you write a review on the website that you bought it from. Reviews help authors with their writing.

Connect with Me Online

Twitter:

http://www.twitter.com/@juliedayauth

or

Facebook:

http://facebook.com/JulieDay

My website:

http://www.julieaday.co.uk

My blog:

http://www.julieaday.blogspot.co.uk

Other books by Julie Day

<u>The Guardian Angel series for teenagers</u>

The Railway Angel*

The Racing Angel *

The Railracing Angels

The Leaping Angels

The Fire Angels

<u>Mermaid Quest trilogy for 9-12 year-olds</u>

The Quest *

The Vanity Quest *

The Emerald Quest *

* available as an ebook and in print.

Printed in Great Britain
by Amazon

83986033R00144